Narratives
from America

Richard Ronan

Narratives
from America

Dragon Gate, Inc. / Port Townsend

Grateful acknowledgment is made to the editors of the following
periodicals in which some of these poems were first published:
Buffalo Gnats: "Provincetown"
U.S. One Worksheets: "The Pickerel"
Hanging Loose: "The Beekeeper's Sister"
American Poetry Review: "Seated Nude," "Fools"
Plum #4: "A Place in the Family"
Ais Eiri: "Easter Crossing"
Poet Lore: "In the Season of the Rutting Moon"

The author is grateful to the New Jersey State Council on the Arts
for a grant which enabled him to complete work on many of these
poems.

First printing, 1982
Library of Congress #81-67639
ISBN 0-937872-04-0
ISBN 0-937872-05-9 (paperbound)

Published by Dragon Gate, Inc., 508 Lincoln Street, Port
Townsend, Washington 98368.

Contents

Introduction

A story houses us. Often more utterly than does our flesh.

I do not mean just the collected wake of events accruing
and intersecting into a kind of minor history; rather the
revelation of these events in the realm of conscious
meaning. This is our story. Each of us may follow this or
flee from it. In either case we make a pattern in space, one
beginning in a given time and one that is in its relentless
design beautiful.

We all live in this way: in a story, in and out of place; living
and dying in this way, speaking in search and prevention of
ourselves, in places and alien to them, given to and taken
from a family, suspecting, betraying and worshiping the
great space that dwells within the story and the storyteller.

This, taken all together, is what I understand as America.

*

The poems in this book are not true. At least they are not
autobiography, or even biography, certainly not the
biography of one person or of one family. The voices here,
like the times and places, are multiple and operate toward

purposes simpler than biography.

What is true is the landscape. And the houses. Most of the poems take place in New England, many in the lake regions of Maine. Some occur in Northern California, several in the Midwest. Others happen, in part, in India, Viet Nam and Ireland. One at midpoint in the Atlantic.

They are the result of thirty-odd years of living in many places in America and wondering why.

I've come to understand this: that one's voice and story, the myth and history of one's country and culture are of a piece—and that if one does not regularly find meaning in some part of this large process, then it is pointless and, at last, hugely dangerous.

This is what I've come to understand as the function of narrative.

pour Sylvie

S'il y a un cercle
qui nous embrasse tous
c'est ta main qui y est restée
toute ma vie.

One might almost describe it as a living being that uses man only as a nutrient medium employing his capacities according to its own laws . . .

Its power to stir is derived from the symbolic value of our native land . . . the *participation mystique* of primitive man with the soil on which he dwells, and which contains the spirit of his ancestors . . .

On the Relation of Analytic Psychology to Poetry, Carl Jung

One of the lies would make it out that nothing
Ever presents itself before us twice.
Where would we be at last if that were so?
Our very life depends on everything's
Recurring till we answer from within.

from "Snow," Robert Frost

Narratives
from America

Fools

If he weren't my brother, I'd have thought
him homely, but since they said we
resembled each other, I wasn't likely
to follow that notion far. So, things
standing thus, I just thought of him
as *plain*. *And* as a fool. Certainly,
he drove a team like a fool, and lived
like one, too, most of the time.
Unstable as water, brittle as ice,
he'd never prosper, they said; never
live to have sons.
I largely didn't care for his lost sons,
and if he did kill himself with
a team wagon and a tree, well,
so would he me,
and the storyteller would go where
the story had gone, and there's a kind
of comfort in that: the comfort, at least,
in not being left out of the one tale
you told with your very heart's blood
and your hands.
Besides, I wasn't just a sister;
I was a rudder, a stone ballast in the hull.

His anchor, he said, forgotten maybe,
left hanging in the last mad turn
of a race around the bay.
For my weight alone, if not for my
soul's sake, he'd not drown either of us,
he told me. I neither believed nor
doubted it; it was just beside the point.

There were others, brothers and sisters,
and also aunts and cousins commuting
through their fields to ours. The society
of them was a constant matter
of interference, for Bill and I had
our *bond*, you know; were in love with
the same madness. Maybe we sought
deliberately to be disinherited,
or sought, more properly, to escape
the house and cabbage rows of inheritance—
the cousins and aunts, the heavy cows—
and flee. Flee away.
I asked him once what it was
that made him so bad.
He said, The moon, and laughed.
And then said—softly, sweetly, like
a boy all in love, *You*, Pet, it's you;
I always know you're watchin'.

Well, I ask you now, is this fleeing one's kith,
really is it? Is it dancing up a birch
and off its top into the black air?
I mean, is this sort of thing actual escape
from this world? Or is it longing for
the others?
That's a great difference to think about,

isn't it? But a difference neither of us,
and no one else in the house, would ever grant us.
Well, no, that's not fair;
maybe Ella did,
but she was so old, so close to dropping
her bones in the clover
while stumbling down to the lake,
that it wasn't fair either to say
she really *knew* what she knew.
But surely it cheered her
in whatever way she understood it
when Bill did something daft.
Wasn't it her who stared like a baby
at the ice block he pulled out of the lake
and left on the kitchen stove—
and it was two, three-foot thick, doubtless?
And wasn't it her who saw
the red leaves trapped there
from last autumn? And didn't she
cry with joy at it for whatever were
her reasons?
Still, we were largely as alone as Cain
when it came to the family; and in their
eyes, bad as sin—maybe even
in our own eyes too. Though I wasn't
wholly sure I'd ever damn Bill to burn
for what they said was his great wickedness.
I might admit my own blackheart
and let a voice beg for salt and thorns
for my deep offenses, but I was not,
and *still* am not, convinced that
my brother, my dear mad soul, was
possessed of any demon but himself.
That jinn, that hot red boy-fire

was life entire to me, the very breath
in my lungs. And I say this, a far bigger fool
than he, since it was, I'll tell you now,
my brother's avowed purpose to kill me—
preferably with some cleverness
that would reach the general ear
and bring him via rhyme
to county fame. Evidently, I didn't mind.

The first time he almost succeeded in his task
was when he had me roast the chestnuts
and they blew off the oven door,
nearly staving in my chest.
The second involved eating
chokeberries till my insides puckered
and my mouth slammed shut, like
the parlor door.
The attempts continued all throughout
childhood, with no real malice; in fact,
with only an entertained and casual
interest on both our parts.
At ten, you can't truly dream of death;
(at twenty-two, of course, you can think of nothing
else).
So perhaps it was wise that we did in
the fascination early and got ourselves wise
to the flat nothing that dying slow
or bloodily brings to its converts.
We'd not die with expectations,
in any case, for either heaven or hell
or anywhere else. Well,
no. Maybe for *mulch*. We both had
a great reverence for mulch. And for the
great power of mulch to translate rot

into roses. We expected *that* much, I'll admit:
to be rendered into mulch. And that's not
an entirely foolish expectation,
all in all, is it?

Billy's last attempt upon me
came in winter. An easy time to slay,
you'd think; an easy time to be slain.
But, like every other act of his,
this also wasn't easy: the *device* was all
to him. I think he'd have been embarrassed
if it were easy, or if he'd killed me
by accident and not by art.
I'm sure, in any case, that he thought
too much of me to put me out
uninterestingly: what really would
be the point to it then?
We were iceboating,
and he caught every nasty wind on the lake:
the ones from Blue Hill, the ones white
and riotous from Canada, even the local
snarls that turned spits on the lake.
Oh, and what he could do with
a sail and the cold, fast air!
Had I less love for him, I'd have
died of fright right then.
But no, that'd not be fair.
We careened down to the Jefferson
end of the lake and then he suddenly pointed
toward the frail town, shouting,
Look there, Pet!
In the distance, I could see the bow bridge.
The lake end went under it,
narrowed itself down to a canal

that carried you to the market wharf.
From the bridge's lip, huge icicles hung,
so many and so thick that they all but
closed the passage underneath;
in fact, they hung so low they touched
the ice surface of the lake.
Now, Pet, *off* to market! Billy shouted.
And he jerked the great, dirtied sail
out sidewise, so it bolted out and shot
us forward.
It seemed the winds had only played us before,
for now they were in earnest,
all of them gathered, side by side,
big and small, glazing down
the ice flat toward the small, walled mouth
of the bridge.
He wouldn't stop, of course. Of course, I screamed.
Red Bill howled like a wolf
as we hit the wall of ice like a meteor.
The mast broke off entirely.
Big trunks and limbs of ice flew everywhere.
The hull split open.
But we went through it, damned if he didn't
almost end us both,
but we went through it!
And what was left of our boat slid
with all the grace of a bed-iron
down the canal, until we hit a sunken timber,
spun like a top,
and were thrown up onto the snow
that must have been the
Jefferson shore.
I couldn't breathe; I think I was also blind.
Surely, I felt nothing, only a shaking

that I believed was the soul
riving out of the body.
All around the town was still: we shared
the white death, the town and I, I thought.
And all I heard in the night
was Mad Bill, lying on top of me,
holding my loosened head hard,
like a glass bell,
and whispering wildly,
Oh Pet, how I love you!
Good Christ, girl, how I *love* your ugly face!

The Pickerel

The lake was shaped like
a hand, they say, a great
deep palm and five tangents,
reaching into the greenwood.
At the tip of each, where
the fingers touched land,
were the coves and the long
ropes of the lilies, holding
onto the finger bottoms.
And under where they opened
and shut, the pickerel steered
like logs between their long
tubes.
They were restrained, the
pickerel, unlike the impulsive
stupid bass, the good driven
salmon. They edged their
hard long bodies around the
tendrils and thick mats of
algae, moving only their
eyes and their small buzzing
fins.

Most often we fished at
dusk and on into the night,
mostly in open water,
pulling white perch up into
the moonlight, but sometimes
we slid into the coves
with our lanterns out,
our hearts muffled, and dropped
a line into the brown debris
where the pickerel hung,
fanning their sides.
I know about them, like
I know about the egg that
filled my mother's belly until
it was my brother; you do know
some things that way.
But there's a clearer reason,
too: one night when I was
nine, we'd caught a pickerel.
My father had wrestled his line
for half an hour, slowly pulling
the creature out of the tangled
maze below us. It looked like
something prehistoric, lying
on the bottom of the boat—
especially under my weak
flashlight—heaving its white
belly while it drowned in the
air.
When I thought it was dazed,
I asked my father if we
could put it back; it was
too bony to eat and it
seemed wrong to, anyway.

Besides, I had seen it and
that was what I wanted:
to *see* it.
My father was just a warm shape
at the other end of
the boat, the coal of his
cigarette rising and falling
as he breathed. He said,
Yes.
But when I reached for the fish
it wasn't dazed at all—
or maybe it just came to life
suddenly when it
found itself in my hands.
Instead, it jumped and
made a sound—a clicking
of its bones, I think—
and pushed its skin out
so that all its fins and hard scales,
its awful bony jaws
opened out
and dug into my
hands.
I cried out once and then
clamped shut like a jar.
My father had the big
flashlight on. I was
bleeding in his light.
Look, look, he said. Look,
(so quietly you could hear
everything, even your own heart)
if you do anything,
it might bolt and tear you.
I nodded. The air was turning

white around me.
It'll go limp soon when it
dies, he said, you'll feel it,
don't move around.
I nodded again. Does it
hurt bad? he said.
I didn't say anything.
I sat on the wood seat,
as rigid as a pole,
the claws inching numbly up
my arms toward my face, prickling
like sleet.

We sat so still you couldn't
even count.
There were mosquitoes hovering
overhead. Bass slapped at
the surface now and then.
The pain got wider, duller,
became like a sail, its ties
cut, flapping loose.
Then I felt a breeze come off
the big lake, breathing down
the thin finger, mouthing
the sweat around my eyes.
The fish bolted once
and I thought I'd die it
hurt so much. Then nothing.
No white. No dark. It felt
dead. It felt like it had
gotten to my door and
knocked on it, knocked on it
all the while it drowned
without its water.

I don't know how long
it took afterwards for it
to relax its grip, slip the
hundred claws out of their
slots in my hands; I was
too dizzy.
I felt my father standing
up in the boat and heard the
swoosh of him swinging
once, a heavy swing, as if
he were punching the air.
The sound of a splash came
back at us from far away.
He let a long breath out of
his body.
I just sat there on the wood,
waiting, the mast in my spine
like ice, just waiting, the lilies
quivering their white
lips, waiting as the breeze
came again from the big lake
and rippled the face of the small
dark cove.

Mother and Child

I told her she'd waited for the apple blossoms.
She said she had; laughed, Who'd have a baby
amid bare branches? True, I said, and timely
hesitation, Sister, considerate of seasons
to wait for the sweetest session to take
to the couch and deliver within the gush,
the scented weeks of spring.
But the apple flowers came and went:
she was late, first two, then three weeks,
more.
We were sure it had been miscounted
at the outset; were convinced of it
when the apple pips showed through, tiny,
yellow, green. It made the everyday
awaited, expectant, watched, timed.
We walked in awareness of walking,
of where and of what the hour was;
walked, then sat awhile
in the gazebo or at the picnic table
in the orchard. Mostly, we walked
by the brook—not the steep side,
the low one; I made certain of that,
without saying it was something

to be considered.
Despite her bad step, she was still
the woman she always was and not one
to be over-accommodated;
she was my sister, always that bond
and wordlessness, always that.

One afternoon, she spoke for a long time.
Brother, she said, do you remember *often*?
Or *much*?
I said I didn't know.
Ah well, I don't usually, she said,
but in the last dozen days, I've been
like a spectator at an inner theater,
watching a play—or tableaux rather,
stilled fragments.
I said, to be sure, it was the pregnancy.
She twilled the lilac spray; smiled.
Buttonhooks, she told me earnestly.
Buttonhooks?
Buttonhooks. Do you remember when
we were young, mother's *buttonhooks*?
And her *shoes*? And for that matter
the sleigh the Olsons had with the bells on it?
Yes, I did; I did recall it.
And Mother, she sighed, my Lord, Mother!
You'd never dream nor think now
the woman suckled wolves and ate raw meat.
She was a terror, wasn't she?
I've thought of her for weeks,
all out of turn: her hair gray, then black,
then streaked with single strands,
the first ones that whitened.
And her hairbrush, Brother. And pulling

out the rat of broken *hair*.
How I hated to brush her hair.
And she *always* had me do it; you escaped
to the root cellar, I'm sure.
Oh the tangle in the bristles and around
my fingers! That was the worst.
I prickle even now to think of it.

She looked down at the water.
I said nothing.
And her sewing box? Do you remember that?
Then she laughed, This must be madness
to listen to. My dear, bear with me,
though I'll not bring it to any sense, I fear.
Things! she said, amused still, *things*.
Yes, kettles. The well ladle, the one
chained to the well stones.
And that lava-like iron pot she had on
the back of the wood stove, *eternally*.
She closed her eyes.
Her in a croquet skirt! Yes, her jewelry
box. And her hats! Oh, her *hats*, Brother,
most of all the one with the pinioned swallow
nailed onto it, the one we called The Pigeon Hat!
She laughed out loud and long, until she wept.
I was afraid for her, but it was so infectious
that I went with it and we were mad as bees,
the two of us, howling till we could only hoot.
I'll deliver right here, she roared, oh my dear,
if I live at all, I will.
And will you *ever* forget the day
I took the butter-brick and buttered
the kitchen floor? Good Jesus,
she was like a thing possessed

when she found me behind the wood pile
and the sink, skidding the lids
to canning jars across that treacherous
slick expanse I'd privately rendered
into a sheet of ice.
Oh Lord—and I can't think *why* I did it,
can you? What six-year-old bit of deducing
led to such a crime?
Then she sat stick-straight upright, Oh *no,*
I *do* remember it!
And she was off again, flailing
and hawing like a jackass; I thought
she'd roll off the bank and drown
in the six inches of water before either
one of us was done laughing and fit
to take air.
Then she grabbed her belly and stilled herself
with effort, leaned into me and said,
Mice,
gasped again and thundered,
It was mice, my dear!
Ma'd said to me
at supper the night before that the mice
were making free in her crisp kitchen
and no amount of cats and traps
had stopped them. So—
clearheaded from birth,
I *buttered* the whole and holy floor
of her kingdom. Clearly, *that* would make
a micey foray at the flour, an attack
upon the breadbox, a very chancy
bit of adventure.
I remember I clearly envisioned
the full raft of them, desperate,

running like watch wheels in place
on the perfect lard I'd made of the underfoot:
mad squeaks, much animation, and not
an *inch's* advance!
We would have only to pick them up
by the tails, salt them a bit for luck,
and drop them down a waiting cat's
throat.
Oh, soul of mine, there was *reason* to it
after all, I see.
And how was I to know that we, the cats,
and all things upright, were to fare no better
than the lowly mice—worse, in fact—
trying to make tracks across that sea
of grease?

We laughed for a long while.
Oh, she was wild; I'm sure
the gray hairs started then and there.
Oh me, what a temper.
And often *mean*, don't you think?
I shrugged. She looked at me quietly,
Mostly mean to *you*, my dear.
Ah yes, you knew her and she *knew* you did.
She knew you read the back of her head
and she used it. As for me,
well, I never thought to know her,
it never occurred to me till later on.
I never stopped to consider her response
to the things I did. I just blundered in
on open impulse and high winds,
as cheerful as a cow in the crib.
And as *dumb*, I fear.
No, well, no, maybe not dumb

but plenty *deaf*, Brother, plenty deaf.
I laughed.
She made a face.
I said, A pain?
A cramp; the boy's heard me talking
and, since he's not only *my* son,
he's gleaned some wisdom from it.
Plainly, Brother, the child's *chosen* not to appear
until full-grown and larger than the issue
of his mother's spleen, her moods,
her spirit daft as weather.
She smiled and put a bit
of the lilac behind my ear.
And *do* you remember the post cards from—
oh, who *was* it was in France when
we were children?
I don't remember, I said.
And those double picture cards
for the stereopticon; I loved them.
Let's see, what else?
She thought, searched the trees overhead.
It was late afternoon.
Another day waited and weighed and no event.
But a fine day, nonetheless, a sweet one.
And the hen that roosted in the hall closet
in Uncle's hat?
I told her I remembered that well enough.
And—
she thought back, then gave it up—
Oh, a thousand things, countless things.
I nodded.
It grew quiet.
The buzz of the insects was loud,
a cicada clacking off in the distance.

I had a dream, I told her at last—
that I was born again.
She said nothing, smiled, toyed with
her flower stem.
Yes, I said, We—you and I—were running
down the hill from the well to the house
and we both fell.
I heard you say, God, my water's broken.
And indeed it had; we were both
soaking wet; everything around us
was also. We stood up, drenched,
our clothes stained with grass.
You were flat-bellied once more
and were asking me, *Are you all right?*
Are you all right? But
I was concerned about *you*.
Where was the baby? How did you come
to be so slender?

And then I realized
it was *me*:
I was the baby,
but not the baby, really.
It was just that it was me
who had just been born.
And I said to you in the dream,
I have ever been convinced of splendor.
And the wound. Convince me, Sister,
of the kindly now.
And you took my head in your hands,
then put my ear to your breast.
I heard your heart thudding regularly,
evenly.

And I knew you would never hurt me . . .

It was still.
I lowered my eyes because I felt ashamed.
She said nothing,
only took my face in her long hands
and stared into it, into my eyes, all the while
shaking her head, saying nothing,
wordless and present
and sweet.

Vista Point

I dreamed Dori and the baby
were in the kitchen and it was so sunny
that the sky was all stiff and brittle.
Then the goldfish in the bowl on the table
went wild and jumped out of their water.
Dori ran with the baby into the park,
while the earth split up in chunks
and big palm trees sunk straight down
without swaying, just like phone poles
dropped into water.
Everyone was screaming.
The sky broke like windshield glass
and where the blue pieces fell away
there was the most brilliant white light
behind the sky: it was
so beautiful that I cried.

Lately I've been wondering a lot.
Not about anything in particular—
not looking for meaning in the cosmos
or anything like that, I've done enough
of that—but wondering about
little things that don't amount to much.

And the wondering doesn't go anywhere,
I just don't know about it.
Sometimes I'm working
and my boss gets crazy about, say,
building the front to this or that
old wreck with wooden plugs and glue
instead of nails. Or sometimes
laying on top of Dori in bed—
once I just laid there for an hour,
watching my seed, in my mind,
seeing it in her,
like a small, eager river,
glowing white inside her—but
a river with a beginning and an end,
just a piece of a river.

I love her more than I can say—
there's no one else'll ever do—
but there's something else
or *things* else
that I don't even call by name
that come on me.
Sometimes in the truck after work
I park at the lookout
on the way back to the city and stare
at the sun going under the ledge of seawater.
And it's like my body rebels and wants
to go after it. I'm like a seabird
whose leash is tied to it, who follows it
at night and pulls it up before dawn.
And I just punch the roof of the cab—
by now it's got dents all over;
looks like a hail storm's beaten it in.
I feel so *caught*

in the things that *can* be—
some dragonfly in amber—and *called*
also by the things that *can't* be,
a man with feet
and no place for them.
If I didn't have fists then,
I think I'd just die . . .
I don't know, I love my wife,
love my son,
but there's a plastic tether
maybe, made of time and place,
that I'm always stretching, pulling at.
I sometimes think if I went off
after the sun,
I'd *not* burn up there; I'd be
some kind of fire in my own right.

I have a private ambition:
to build a staircase in a Swiss town maybe
or in some southern church back home
where the miraculous still comes
home from the swamp—
a spiral staircase, much like a barber pole,
and one made without a single nail or joint,
inexplicably made so that no one piece
could have been done
without all the others first being finished.
A puzzle and a miracle I want it to be.
And then when it's done, I plan to leave
the clapboard town by night,
like St. Joseph, on a mule maybe,
or just afoot with sandals,
never having spoken to anyone,
rector or wives,

leaving them each to wonder
what visitor it was who made this
and if, oh, *if* they dare to climb the stairs
and if the treads would make them holy.

I'd like to tell the baby about this,
but he's like the fish sometimes,
steering around the chairs like he was
in corkscrew grass. If he could
he'd uproot it all, let it float: tight, white roots
all naked; chairs, rugs, me, lying sidelong
on the ceiling.
He likes the fish; I show them to him
all the time. I show him the lime tree
on the sill. I show him my picture
of the earth,
the lapis-like mix of the world
seen from above,
looking like an ear-jewel, a marble,
another eye, staring placidly back.
He kicks like a turtle at it.
I wanted to have him with me
at the lookout today after work.
There were a lot of picture-takers
there today, all squinting into a lens
for a picture of the seal herd on the rocks,
all shooting right into the sun.
They don't bother me anymore. I know they come
and go home to long pants
and high position. They only travel
in order to go back and throw whale fins
up onto their walls for whatever neighbors
they have in their high-rises on the Loop.
To me they're just little figures

against the sunset,
going down to L.A., going up to Eugene.
They never stay away from the motels
so near to dark.

I was thinking about the baby.
The sun turned a lemon color, then
almost colorless; and the cliffs
turned a brass color, the sky a bird-like gray. ›
The baby is eighteen months old;
he would have liked it.
When I was there alone,
a row of pelicans flew by. Seven of them.
Just above the horizon,
not touching the sun at all,
as if they'd be burnt by it.
And all at once, I just went wild—
a sort of cold wildness I'd never felt before—
that shook me as if I was freezing.
I was standing all alone
on the cliff edge, taking the peaches,
one by one, out of the crate
I had in the bed of the pickup,
and I was throwing them one at a time
at the sun,
cursing nonsense at it and crying
like a baby, the whole while
it sunk down,
down to Japan and China, to Rome
and all those places they take pictures of.

The fog came in.
I needed the headlights
it was so dark when I left,

the empty crate rattling in the back.
Oh Dori, Dori,
woman, I love you best and forever,
but there's ambition in me
which we all need to fear.

Flower and Stone

We don't know if he subsists
on a diet of lilies alone,
but so it *seems* to us
as we come to and from the house
and find him grousing incommunicable
beneath the privet;
God knows Brother's odd.
He told Fanny the Orientals eat them cooked
—I mean the lilies, not the hedges—
but that he finds *that* too cruel.
Instead, he elects to swallow
the gay heads fresh and whole
as would a dim cow—and he's become
about as welcome as a sudden cow
at picnic.

For a week after he told her,
Fanny spent the time eyes shut,
head back, holding the yellowy things
by tips over her open mouth,
while Betty dared and giddied her
to push them in; she never did.
All she ever ate was stray pollen

and the dust of the air,
but then Fanny has seemed
to dwell quite a lot on air
and Betty all too much on collusion.

Those of us who pay attention at all,
or who are still willing to talk about it,
will tell you we've found him everywhere,
adventuring on blossoms.
And that talking gets you nowhere with him.
Not now, at least: he's as deaf as
a bluebell and as common an occurrence
on the hill.
For a time, you could have dragged
him home by the belt, but no more.
After his novitiate with mere day lilies,
he fell to a wild youth of red tulip-taking,
then browsed forth into other fields:
public gardens, window boxes.
Scenes occurred which I'll leave at rest
like the new wounds they are.
I'll only say he's more *discreet* now.
And more exotic, wholly gone
to fields farther flung than those
we all knew. No more bunchberry blooms;
cinquefoil's behind him.
Now he spends his nights in sugar maples
harvesting cheekfuls of a colorlessness
which we barely knew existed there;
and by dawn, is down with the spider paws
of dewdrop blooms,
mouthing the yellow foot of a lady's slipper.

Still, I have to say I'm grateful:

he isn't ravenous anymore.
Nor does he still impose upon our neighbors
much by eating their lawns.
So at last what can we do but sit
with remnant nerves and some small
dignity
and endure the lunatic's legend
he's wrought for us and himself;
endure his chewing through the unowned woods,
odd and ever odder bits of bloomery
vanishing into his eager jowls;
endure as the sister of legend,
the sibling of the son
who ate the countryside,
the daughter of a mother who was frightened,
clearly, by locusts.
But, *damn*,
why doesn't he cane a chair
or restring the screens,
instead of inhaling the landscape like he does?
Small infamy at the grocer's
is not what I was born to.
And more maddening still
is the silence he leaves us in
and the questions that echo in it:
what does this mean?
Where will this lead? Oh,
does this say he'll never marry?
Will we always need to fear
for a poor girl's fist of mock orange
and whether it will reduce Brother
to the graces of a truffle pig?
We don't know.
Mainly because he is more often out

licking the iris than he is on civil and solid
ground
with those members of the house
who acknowledge that he still exists.
And surely none of us is much willing
to burrow through the blackberry hedge
to interview this apostle of the petal
and secret tubs of honey—
all of which is to roundabout say
that we don't know *why*
he eats flowers,
nor why he does nothing *but*
eat flowers.
We are a family kept ignorant
and yet blamed.

Yes, we sent the Reverend once,
poor worm,
only to have him dragged
by his fraying cuff through the spring wood
to the bay bog
where he was subjected
to a little pagan rite,
involving a swamp lily, my brother
and some lunatic divinity of the mud.
When Brother stuffed
the pink thing down his throat,
our cleric bolted, shrieked, *Papist*!
and ran—well, slogged, I guess—
his way back swiftly to clapboard
and reason.
So it's not likely that the good Reverend
will much inquire into Brother's habits
farther than he has.

Of course, *I* followed him;
outright spying, and, what's more,
with vengeance.
I *swore* I wouldn't; I swore he'd
have to come to breakfast if he was
to speak to me;
that I'd never stoop to the altitude
of a bluet and catch *his* eye.
But I did.
This was on the morning—in fact,
the dawn—in which the azalea bloomed
its ruby wash across the cellar footing,
for all the good it did.
By quarter to six,
half of each bush was neatly deflowered;
right down the middle of each globe he'd cut,
clean as a scythe,
much like the earth is said to be halved
by night when witnessed from above.
Well,
I stood agog there
for some minutes, and then awoke to sense
and swiftly fled; I needed only a moment
to imagine the breakfast of tigers
that would ensue
when the others came out to down
their morning cups of tea
and blew out their teeth instead
to see the shrubs begobbled.

I went strictly with purpose: to find
Brother and thrash him witless
for the truncated spring.

And I found him soon enough—
no, he hadn't exactly left a telling trail
of chewed azalea flesh
that tiptoed to his lair,
but neither had he run with caution.
Clearly, he'd already advanced
with the disease past shame.
He was without ruth,
as rude, cheerful and amoral
as the unchristian wind.
And, more to the point, as clumsy
as a moose: he was easy to track.

I found him down at the lake,
up to his knees and arrayed in mud,
surrounded by the white and static lilies,
the violent spatterdock.
He had his trousers rolled up (I recall
that this told me he wasn't *as* far gone
as I'd feared),
shirt off, hat on, and making
his selection off the face of the cove,
a madman at a sunken market.
I was about to throw my rocks at him
one by one—surely some
would knock his silly hat off
and raise an egg on him.
But then I saw his face and stayed
my arm.
It was, I think I'd have to say, *transfigured*
and ever so still,
so full of the lake and the slow travel of cloud
overhead,
so full that the rock ached

to be let down again and I had to sit
in the brush and watch him.
It was like I'd imagine a play to be:
him orderly as a priest,
moving to a music you would
hear at church,
an in-and-out sort of thing,
the content of the heart turned out
and worn like a coat; him in the lake,
the lake in his eyes, the heart floating overhead
all white and whiteness.
Well, I don't know,
I don't know *which* way it was now.
I mean, I *know* he ate the flower, yes,
but I know it no better than I'd know
what two mirrors would do
to face each other with no one in between.
It seems *as* likely now to remember it
that it was *him* who entered the *flower*,
him who walked down its round corridor
to the yellow crown
and whatever room or arbor hung with seed
it offered at its center.

It seems I've gotten it backwards.
Well, it makes little difference;
or, at best, the difference swings on
hinges other than these.
Brother's his own agent now
as far as I'm concerned.
Truly, I no longer notice much
what he's drawn to do—or eat—
out on the earth.
Nor do I any longer worry it.

He is, I guess, a man
of as many sins and failures
as any other, none of them significant
nor unheard of.
The same may be said of his
and others' virtues.

And, well, this:
I still have one of the rocks
I was going to throw at him.
It sleeps in an upper drawer
with my linens,
as still as my only secret.
Every morning I am drawn to look at it,
there abed with my silks.
And I have to laugh
to myself, my drawers, the room,
my reasonable nighties: Oh
Sister, you are, you know, as mad
as he is.

In the Season
of the Rutting Moon

She's gone and seen her face is what she's done.
I know her like myself and she's gone and seen
her face, I tell you—a woman who's seen
herself only twice before: once at our joining
when she'd run off in her white skins and beads
to the lake because she knew it was a windless
day and her last as a child.
As I waited at her father's long house,
she climbed a willow and crawled out
over the water, squinted in. I don't know
what good view she had of herself, but it seemed
to settle her.
In any case, we wedded. She's been a good wife.
I a fair man to her.
The other time was when our first boy was sick,
asleep in her arms, where she sat outside
by the door, staring into the woods,
praying. I know she prayed to that red and black
and white bird-thing she says hasn't a name
she can ever speak.
The boy breathed hard in his fever sleep
and made a bubble of spit between his lips.
She saw her face then too, for a minute maybe,

before it broke and the boy breathed in again,
maybe easier. She said it was easier.
I guess she knew.
And now again,
again by the lake. Now that we've got
a darker sky, and there are few leaves
to confuse the water's surface. She reached
for a stick on the bottom to drag the clothes
she'd just washed, and there was her face again,
forty years older, a good leathern face
I've never ceased to see
and think was fine.

Since then she's been silent,
sitting off on the ridge
above the copper-colored river,
not eating, no. I sit behind her
further up the ridge; she doesn't hear me
when I talk to her.
I thought she was afraid, convinced this was
her last season, the last of a hundred autumns;
and time for her to count
the leaves by tree and kind,
the stars by color—yes, she can still see
a blue star from a red with her little gray eyes,
far better than I can, far better than I ever could.
She sits there still,
like the dark ground itself
and I know I've heard her mumble
that blessing-song she always sang to the boys,
moving her hands like she was sowing grain.
But to whom now?
To what does she give it?
The animals? The air?

Something in my lungs says she strives
to make things fertile,
to give herself over to the mosses,
to make a mumble-song that steps out
of its skirts and climbs the blue staircase
she believes in
to the sun.

It's not your time, *woman, get that through*
your thick Leni head.
Nor is it mine, damn you!
I run down and tell her this every day.
I tell her spine; it's been a full week
she's not even looked up at me.
She stares out, counts some fraction
of light on some small river rock
as the water runs its rust and iciness over.
Maybe she counts her breath—I tell you
it's the only time in forty years
I've felt she wasn't mine, that she wasn't
even my wife.

Is it the old face, tell me?
It's the same face I've been chewing meat with
for decades, squaw.
What can it mean, after so long, tell me?
I said that at first. But no,
no, it's not the face. It was. To begin with,
it was.
I should have gone right away to her
and told her if the damned river
made her into an old woman
she could just go on looking at the blue bride
in my old eyes.

But I didn't. I don't know why.
I just didn't. And in the time it took
to stall, she'd lapsed,
gone on past the fear of death and the shock—
oh, I know the shock, finding your eyes
are yellowed, your cheeks like the clay pit
in summer.
And by now, it's not just that. I know her.
No, she's gone past it, gone right beyond
the old face, and just as clear past
the face of the bride, upside-down, white-skinned
in the willow tree.

She's with the bird-thing.
That's what it *is*, you know: a face
that never was one, never will be;
and a place where her old silence can shed me
like a lap rug.
I know her; I know her well. But now
I also know her absences.

Oh, old madame, Lady Still-Waters,
girl I took to wife; oh woman,
if your silence has a heart, if it counts a beat
in human time,
you'll not leave me here in autumn,
nor when the air is birdless,
the ground the color of your old Leni hair.

The Scholar

for Ben

The old man who planted these oaks
had, in his youth, taken the name
Malachi—or at least it was repeated
that he did; perhaps it was true.
The name is in the old part of the book
and we can ask what it means,
but we can no longer guess at
how it was true, or even for whom,
or if it was a flat-faced sort of truth
or one stood on its head and meant
to mean its own inverse.
But it's likely that the name-taking
was a joke, a private one
that an isolate soul had made
with his faceless God, or maybe one
had by that same soul on the faceless
mob of onlookers to that discourse.
Still it's too late now to truly tell much
about his name; what might have
been ours is lost under those needs
which govern what is remembered,
what let go by.
Consider: a man who was,

while alive, half-forgotten,
the other half unnoticed, whose
substance was later summed
in the general mind into a myth of trees,
truly, what *can* we know about him?
Not much. Only things such as this:
that he was the only laborer at his
oak task; and though no one survives
to test it with memory, it's still said
he had a mute Indian boy with him,
hired only to carry the sandals he would
never wear. We remember them together,
if at all: one barefoot, the other badly
shod, paralleling a system of stakes
to govern a line northeast/southwest;
together and not knowing each other,
artlessly stitching, bent and
inching along, (at least in legend)
making the wide double row of trees
that stretched from the county road
to the porch of their borrowed home,
a distance just under a mile all told
and one spaced so well that each
oak raised its pin-leafed tent
to finger the neighbor branches,
to let in and out the sky. One other thing
is known: that the old man had been
a monk; had one day left the monk's estate,
his village; left Europe; left the whole
speaking world, in a way, and took
a gardener's service with strangers
whose language he heard but never spoke.
He raised their sons; kept their root
cellars; prayed; planted the mile-long

walk of oaks and passed demurely
out of his own legend into a legendary
arcade of wood instead.
These are the trees that remain to us
even now.

From the third story of the house
you might see the entire corridor of them
spaced out like even steps measured away
from the sill where you sat,
until you swore it bent
with the curve of the earth,
out past thought, past reason,
up to the huge hip of the unseen sea.
In autumn, the far end of the avenue
that met the county highway, being
more northerly, was said to turn
its color a full week before the trees
that flanked the more southern gates of the
house. And for the whole week, they said,
you could sit—if you had the
blank week to do it, or if you could
steal the same hour seven times
at the same stroke out of your teeming week—
you could sit and piecemeal watch
the season burn its minions
on its way southwest, until its largeness
lit up your chin where it rested, contemplative,
on the white sill. But this, too, was only
local legend, or less—maybe only
family legend, perhaps the legend only
of the child whose chin found the hours
to think it all through.
What was truer and *could* be seen

in a single sitting, had you the wit to see
at all, was the yearly habit of the moon,
all full of milk and faceless,
as she took the same track down
the flat sky; sometimes in winter, sometimes
in a hotter season, but always in just
the same way: rising at the northeast end
of the oak run, gathering and growing big
as she walked her way somewhat south
to awe and quiet us
with the advent of a planet
on the family porch. *That* you could watch
and plot out ahead of time, if you could
figure the angles and hours right. It was
a briefer ceremony and a simpler one
and you could divine it better
than you could the purpose
of a whole season or of your cluttered life.
Consider: as a lady without context,
come white and all alone
one night a year
with the rest of the world blacked out
and worshipful; isn't it far easier
to guess at *her* imports than to guess
at your sister's?
Or at the wife who lives beside you
and has a whole calendar of names?
This, some say, is the *gift*
we're given in the moon; that she makes
a miniature of the day, of a whole history,
and mums it out like a mime
for the grave child of her own sort.
And so perhaps were the trees
a gift on this order.

And also the worn image of the male couple
endlessly seeding their mile.

It's true, it was never the monk's house.
But those that had it, didn't have it
long either. It passed a course
through sons and wives of sons
to cousins and nieces and then to other bloods.
And with it the oaks.
They set the new county lines by them.
Some said you could set your watch
by them too, and, if resolute, that
you could also find in its long narrative
your own tree of relations; on it your own
recent history and the very leaf inscribed
with the tale you had to tell.
Twelve boarders for thirty years lived
in the garret of the house
before *that* secret came back to anyone;
and it was only the first of countless such
that waited to be found again by someone.
But no one lived long enough in the world
usually to learn more than the one,
which was simple: that with diligence
you could *see* the world
and its multiple spawn reveal itself,
perhaps through the cycle of a single year,
or in the ordered arcade of the trees,
or in the coming of the moon
to the southern sill
with its pale hosannas. It was
a chosen man who knew this, for it was
a hard realization and it could cost you
something to live past it.

The man who did was odd. And he who
was taken by the other secrets, well,
no one knows what he has to say,
or if he can speak at all of it,
or even if he fully knows he's been
chosen past the rites even of the chosen.

The twelfth boarder was a scholar,
but that had little to do with it.
He was bookish and unpretty, fervent
over things no one would ever think of.
The liberal minds thought him ever the boy
at heart; the tighter minds that he was
outright mad, but at least
privately so. He read Greek; he'd read the Latins,
all of them; he'd read the Great Treatise;
knew the six lines; knew them well.
And they knew him, too;
recognized his touch
on their yellow leather; came to him
like comforting worms to spell him messages.
No one knew it—and it would have tested
the liberal's tolerance to learn it—
but he'd gone six times to Chicago
solely to read; once to New York
for the sake of seeing certain papyruses
that a man otherwise and countlessly dead
had painted in Egypt.
He'd lain with six women for love
of them and one boy for the love of God.
And the only things, besides his books,
that he kept were the formal handkerchiefs
he'd asked each love to kiss
and give him—those veils—and

fifty yarrow twigs that in a dream
they'd all together picked and winnowed
at a Chinaman's grave, in order
to better read the lines
that were whole and the lines
that were, in this life, broken.
No one but these seven friends noticed
his name either.

The oaks slowly captured him, or
at least took his attention away.
Sometimes when he looked up
from his text to consider its subtle meat,
a breeze would rouse itself; teach
its creatures the air; let them die again.
Then the trees, the air, the whole tableland
surrounding, would not stir again
for days. He would wait,
baited for the next motion that the world
outside would make. This inevitably
grew to more than itself; gave itself over;
allowed other, older things
to perform on the stage it set
and then abandoned. The scholar
noticed none of this. Instead, he played,
like the Italian, the English don happy
in Shakespeare's day, giving each tree
a subject in the catalogue
of knowledge, each bough a place in
history, too tediously each leaf—
all to eat the whole of what
was known; to give it permanent
flesh in one man's memory. To *know*,
yes, to know was what he was about;

the gaining entrance to what
was a doubled decade of centuries,
to countless disciplines,
to every dead and deader man's
gleanings; he wished only to know
that book, that page, that word.
Still, he was more modest than,
say, a Francis Bacon; he knew he couldn't
do what had occurred to him to do.
This was plain wise, but he felt
he also knew the *reason* for it too,
and this was just foolish.
It came, he said, from being a Yank,
a stepson to civilization.
What *connection* could he have,
born too late, too westerly?
For years and more than just space,
the flat table of wheat,
this plain of vegetables had fanned out,
blonde and fertile, from the house,
bisected once by the oak line;
and never again, until the mind
broke its heart on the specter of
its own isolation. What was Europe
here in the corn, or Asia? The life
of a wordler who ate no grain?
But the reason
was the thing itself; not that he
was misborn, but that great knowledge
undoes itself; is at best
a toy to the heart, even a dead heart;
leaves the seeker sought,
more like the dog and its tail,
than like a man staring through trees

into emptiness.
And so the more he thought, the further
it failed and in the caverns
its leave-taking left
was only an unlovely man,
seated at a third-story window,
slowly panicking
in a nearly-square county,
watching a world of men and seasons
that had but barely made its presence
felt on him, except once, twice—
well, perhaps the full seven times that
he ate his way through sweat
to the flesh-gates that house our God.

It was at this time that he found the baby.
For days beforehand, his breathing had
been poor, a slow rasp, like a saw
pulling up out of wood, wet wood in fact,
which had swelled on the saw and
rusted it a bit. It was like smoke,
he said, like a snake in the throat.
He sat at the window hauling breath;
took to staring down the arcade, mindless
for hours at a time. It is like breathing
your own blood, he said at last.
There was no weather, no noticeable
color to things. The light was neutered,
no temperature clear.
The result of this was stillness—
no, *absence*, genuine absence,
spreading like a head
of low cloud upon the whole state.

Nothing had called him to the child,
maybe dim impulse, only clear enough
to send him laboring
through his laundry supposedly searching
for a tin of camphor; he came, instead,
upon a baby's face. It was awake,
silent, indeed the source of the
gathering stillness around him.
It was moist, naked; the room entirely
too cold for it. It did nothing
but stare; refused nourishment from
his spoon; nor would it respond to any
colored thing he waved at it.
It only caught and possessed his eye.
That was its only talent; it seemed
its only need, a silent staring that
glowed from its face.

The child came from nowhere. No woman
in the house or in town, wed or otherwise,
had been pregnant. And he did notice
a mother-to-be; had always had
a bachelor's sense of them;
often knew their plural secret
before they themselves did.
Besides, the babe was not
just thrown by a full-skirted
Christian not seen for three months.
Its eyes were too old,
as were its hands; a month, perhaps
two months old. And the child's body
was too wise in a way, capable of touch,
sentient in its nest of frayed shirts
and thin towels.

He wondered, at first, about its appearance,
its origin, as anyone would. But that
passed quickly, and as the child's silence
and the house's silence wedded the awesome
winter stillness that took the countryside,
it became more a question of who
the child was than a search
for where it had come from.
And to that the infant only stared.

That year the season set in early.
In the wake of its first storm the plains
were useless as glass. Whatever occupation
a whole landscape can be thought to have,
there was no longer any thought of it; the
skin of the earth looked more like
the skin of the moon.
Colorless light took the room,
thrown there off the sky, the disputable
inches of snow that fell often,
uneventfully; fell in and out of time,
a repeating event that effectively removed
any notion of event.
Last clusters of oak leaves hung
like abandoned nests.
The domes were thick, the ground soft.
Everything matted and advanced
a quietude. Nothing had a clock.
It seemed that he huddled all day
over the child to warm it. When he slept,
he did so uneasily with it wedged
between his spare body and the wall.
But this was not greatly warm and he finally
took to stripping naked, holding the also-naked

For weeks, nothing progressed.
They were two fish, half conscious under
a lid of ice. They were written in a lost book
or partially reconceived in a drifting
memory. They were other than they were.
The great stillness came to serve
as a pivot. The man's alterations
wandered undisciplined around it, through it.
The snow fell; things also fell from him;
were driven upwind; accrued into corners.
And all the while, the child lay
like a static pearl in the turning milk.
He thought: this is failure, isn't it,
the realization of failure? He saw
his critics as correct: he *was* mad;
had always been.
This is loneliness, isn't it? he asked.
This is the loss of purpose?
But, at best, it was both what he thought
it was and its opposite, the inversion
of all he'd ever think it to be.

child to his bony chest, then rolling up
in every cloth and blanket in the house.
It seemed that all night
some part of him waked and breathed into
the center of this nest.
The child seemed unaffected. As far
as he could tell, it never slept at all.
It only sometimes clawed softly
at his chest. And of course, it stared.
In the moonlight that fell in clear weather
onto the bed, it often seemed to glow
like the snow itself.

At times, he'd ask questions of the child,
each spaced over several days,
but those days so eroded that
the questions seemed like a straight line
of them, all asked close-heeled:
Oh child, who are you? Child, are you death?
Child, please tell me, are you the madness
they said would take me? Child, are you
my unborn? Child, are you my youth?
Are you love, child, at last? Or love
remembered? Oh child, are you doubt?
And the only answer the infant made
was its small mouth pulling on
his reddened teat, nursing, it seemed,
on his losses, suckling these
as if they were a sugared spigot.
Faith, he'd whisper to his seven loves,
Faith, dears, this is a way
through the thicket of God.
He'd close his eyes; surrender to the child
and drift into a passive season
where the root drank.
Faith, he'd say, give us faith in it.
At night, he'd dream that
he and the child swam through the snow
like fish that dwelt at the depth
of the ocean. They ate ice; they had
their own light.

He woke; he was out in the snow.
It was night. He didn't remember
going out; he'd slept through it.
Yet he had been careful enough
of the child; wrapped it in his clothes;

buttoned it under his greatcoat.
He'd taken an umbrella for its sake,
a lacquered paper one he'd never used
for fear of the town's reaction
against him. But now, at night,
in thick snowfall, no one would be out
walking a farm and, if they were,
they'd not see ten feet before them well.
He only realized where he was when
he heard the sharp snow prickle
the oiled skin of the parasol.
The noise was quite loud in his ear
for a while, but then a felting of snow
gathered on it. Soon there was little
to hear, and as little to see.
Here and there, small episodes left unfinished:
a squirrel torn apart by owls, but
not bloody, rather pastel, in fact
as uncarnal as the objects butchers make
public for lunch; branches downed
by weight; footprints of deer, which had
wandered without food or decision;
a sled's even track pulled across
the walk like the armpiece of a
great cross. Nothing that wasn't on its
way away, nothing present,
only him and his clumsy pushing at the snow,
the child burrowing through woolens
at his chest, the umbrella gathering a roof
above them.

What might have been a walk for lovers,
for mothers revealing the source of blood
to daughters, was now a journey,

and a journey he hardly had the wit to
notice. Vacant, hollow, he lapsed
back to sleep. Something else fought
to walk forward, convinced that he must
remain between the two columns of oak,
that the child must stay warm
inside his coat and that the county road
must surely lie somewhere
in the history of the trees, some part
of a mile ahead.
There was no sense of what he did,
or why, what drove him out into the night.
He half-dreamt that he was
a night-crosser, an expatriot slipping
a border, perhaps sly and dangerous,
between a minute country
and a greater power. But where
the border fell in the snow, or where
fell the wall, the pass, and what features
told the larger country from the lesser—
of these he knew nothing.
The umbrella grew heaped. He stopped
twice for breath; went on.
On the third cease, he felt surely
he was drowning; he fell.
The ground went black.
When he woke again, it was no longer
snowing. The trees had ceased
their company. The plains lay open.
He was at the county road.

The wind dipped here, as it glanced
the plain, and cleared the deep snow
from the junction of the house

and county roads. In the stead of snow
was a sheet of ice, covering over
the intersection, so that it had the face
of a lucid pond or
of a large lake in miniature.
Above, the clouds had broken into heaps.
These opened on a black sky,
a full moon, a minute star. He stared
at the glass surface of the road where
it caught the image of the clouds, the moon
in its oval.

        For a moment, it was a scene,
a frozen portrait framed by the banks of snow:
a ghostly lorry and driver
in furious haste; the horses caught up
in a rear, reins lank, their manes
belled and knotted. The man shouted
some vowel, his whip lashed into
a rat's tail swirl, about to crack.
But it didn't. Nor did the wagon carry
its cargo on. Nor did the horses
come down from their stand. All was still,
an image of commerce halted under ice,
revealed in all its nostriled strain,
its unvisionable beauty.

He turned to the house,
lost in the light and dark of a mile of snow.
The horses drifted off; the clouds overhead
altered, pulling into strips that looked
like rawhide. Then these, too,
became too vague to name
and all that was left on the whole landscape
was a great sadness,

one that had no content or cause,
but only great size. It took no word;
certainly no question. Indeed, it was
like the glass road before him that would
bear no passage but the eye's,
the mind's, or that of the impossible feet
which carry the heart when we've
surrendered all other bearers.
Six other stars opened in the sky.
The sadness passed into fullness,
the fullness into palpable space.
Above, the moon began its walk southward
down the oak road to the house,
large as a platter,
pulling at the snow, the ice,
at all the liquids within him.
The babe suckled at his teat for milk.
Twin rivers of sweat ran down his sides.
For a moment, he recalled
the boy he'd loved had once stood
on his thighs and reached up,
yearning, at the sun
and maybe even beyond the sun.

Seated Nude

She hiked; knew she had to.
Summer last she paced up the
eastern edge of Canada; the year before
up the lower spine of the Appalachian.
This year it was Ireland in the
constant rain.
He understood; also knew that he had to.
He was a greatly hairy man,
smelling like a stale red fur; she
a fine, thin woman who'd become,
in two years, near-wild
with raw halves of beef, cattle storms,
fire and glacial till moving, scratching
across her inside flesh:
all love and rage. She was the first
to say it; she'd talked it all through.
He, too, had talked it through.
They had friends with ears, outlets
for the wobbling sense of futility,
for the moments when the need
to entertain decision reigned; friends
also for when it passed
and only grim circumstance sat

in its sparse corner. They talked through
all the elements, all the feelings
surrounding the elements: the confinement
to the chair, his death from the torso
downward, her life tipped over, dragging
like an oak table caught on a leash,
his embarrassment at being baggage
to himself, to her—
they *knew* themselves and their situation.
It was no one's fault; there was no
apologizing for it, no anger at it.
Such retreat wasn't their province;
they couldn't even borrow it and be fair.
It was their simple *fact* that
they daily faced,
not their points of view, each leaning
in against the other,
not even their great regard
for each other—but fact,
circumstance: their life, unlike most,
became only itself.

He had been a good lover; had
matched her good mind and her good
bony body with a thick lust,
a good sense of who she was.
He'd been short, she taller.
In bed, he liked to climb her.
After the crippling, he did what tongue,
red beard and fingers could do—
and it was considerable, too.
He hauled the listless hips
with a kind of art across her bed,
such that her loss might be less

than the loss of a toy, a seven-inch bat.
It sufficed as distraction.
And through all this vast recompense,
he grew large muscles in the arms and
neck and face. The chest fattened; rose
into cakes. Like a gymnast,
he swung his unresponding legs
through the house on a clever sequence
of rings and dance-bars
that he'd devised for himself.
He seldom fell; she seldom had
clear reason to weep.
And the little deaths
of the heart and the large fall
of meaning in their life were thus
kept in stay, like two wars maintained
on either side a wall.
Still, one night, while she lay
opened to his face and fierce arms,
she knew suddenly—and it is sometimes
only suddenness can push things through
to be known at all—
that he was weeping
in his labors at her; she sensed
more than felt the tears
fall through both their sweats
and bead up their salt, their sand,
inside her rednesses:
she had to walk.
She knew then that she had to walk
great distances.

The family had come from Ireland,
evolved its twilled thread of generations

into a design, like the design
we'd see in nerves.
And in pacing back through that
progress, she found a whole
'world-behind-the-mirror'
of duplicates and equivalents—
small caches of foreign cousins,
removed twice and living in towns
or on stone-rut farms—
all repeatable milk-faces that,
like their American matches,
blemished too easily; aged too quick.
It all seemed like an album
read backwards, a Chinese history,
the point of it found not in its pinnacle
but in its founding,
in the incepted seed
that was and always had been
the full-blown tree.
In many ways it was a grim and verdant
landscape, the medieval green
half-taken from the sea encroaching;
half, she said, drawn out of some
forty shades of mold.
Too wet, the sky hung as heavy as earth;
the land as porous as the air.
The heart hung: a cupboard left open.
All she saw was heavy with itself.
She walked northwest
across grassland, stone,
until, at last, the fog and sea-breath,
the tight, wet hills sliding down
with periwinkle,
became a feeling—the national feeling,

she insisted—and a simple one: a fear
of the flesh, of the lung, the terrible
sense that any heart that beat
was a heart black with lust, with loss,
and one better off not beating at all;
the sense that the only peace
one ever saw, hovering over this damp earth,
came when one saw a piece of poor flesh
surrender, dry, and die.
She wondered with the arrival at every town
what had come down the genes
and across the sea to her, what she'd
inherited through marriages.
At Limerick, she arrived in the midst
of a wake—a dim uncle, a tall man,
thin like herself, who had always worn
gray—a great storyteller, they told her.
They told her his story.
They also showed her his corpse.
It wore a heavy suit, as his body
seldom had.
There were photographs in the coffin
of him as a boy. Aunts who'd
heard of her grief at home were
pointedly kind; they patted her,
sharing her sorrow like
a milky cup of tea.
They brought the widow to her.
She pressed her grieving fist of beads
into her hands. *Commit yourself
to circumstance*, the woman told her;
there was a great bitterness in her.
You're not a girl anymore, you know.

After this she stayed at inns,
avoiding the relatives. At night,
she read maps; drank stout alone in pubs.
Soon she found she chose to walk
at night; it involved her less
and was without great difficulty.
She had good vision in the dark.
She rarely fell. And when she did
she nearly enjoyed the abrupt break
in her pace,
the momentary drop into a shallow well
of sweetfern; she fell as a child falls
from its own history. In the dark
she saw and longed for no aunt,
only for wood, the surrender to water,
dark earth, to the dog in the distance
confused by sheep. The many
blind grasses were as kind as hair,
the many invisible mosses gracious
on their mounds of new rock. And
asleep or awake
she thought continually of his body
in the chair.

At Sligo
the hiking grew arduous. With double the
effort, she threw herself at it;
made a discipline of it, a game of counts.
It became her, or became whatever
part of her that needed a body walking
in sweat to surface itself.
Relieved, she vacated herself.
The walking legs still missed him,
the back felt relieved at being away.

The cheek worried, the foot fled the worryings
again and again; until the body,
taken altogether as a single-purposed
engine, made a green blur of concern,
a blur also of love and longing, of
the entrapment and the four winds that
passed outside their window at home.
She put miles underfoot eroding the hollow
lightness of his chair, his useless sweat,
the maddening, calling smell of it,
the past, once clearly theirs, now
embedded like a metal van in a wall
off in the delimited future—yes, to make
a blur of that *finality*, that endurance,
and of the moonlight, the streetlight,
the daylight, the dark
laying down its smooth and gradual weight
upon his motherish chest,
his shoulders, of his thick throat
and yes! the dead, large man-sac!
The dragging flag of flesh down there
between unspeaking, deaf legs! Yes!
A blur of *that*, God yes! Of that and of
the anger, yes, and of the hated life
and the love of him! Of his pains
and cutting down, of the loss of all and
any meaning in the day, of impossible
necessity! Of daily prevention!
Yes, a blur of all of it—a miasma, God,
that erased that world where only
the cool chair existed
amid the swing of chromium rings
and impossible love.

At Errigal, at dawn, she slept.
She dreamed; it was night at home.
The mercury light fell from the street pole,
the chalk light from the moon.
He sat nude in the chair.
It was oppressively hot.
He was sweating in the dim light.
The aluminum poles, the tacky plastic
pad were wet with it.
The metal chilled the skin of his arm,
his back. She felt the odd blunted
sense of it cooling obliquely
against the back of his thighs,
his legs; the lame sac, the penis
spread out flat on the seat.
It was a feeling like being half
in water.
She was calm in the dream, in Errigal,
the mother of feelings, all in order,
in equipoise.
She reviewed his body, his muscled face;
she knew the man inside.
His thighs were like stone.
The absence in his legs was an aching
in hers.
She felt the vast fever burn behind his eyes.
And knew in the most amazing way
that nothing had changed—nothing.
This was their life, unadorned,
seated in a dream. At once
she felt a great feeling in her;
told herself that she must remember
to straddle his shoulders
when next they met, to trust the center

of her hips to his mouth,
to cradle his big head with her knees
and, while the rings turned silent
in every direction from their ropes,
to give to his teeth
a string of pearls from out of her womb,
while whispering Yes yes
oh Lover yes.

Provincetown

This winter, they tell me, the street
that ran along the waterfront,
like the spine of the town, sank in,
crushing the water pipes beneath it.
This flooded instantly, like an
opened lung, froze almost as fast,
and then lay the whole season
under a run of scratched glass,
growing thicker and whiter daily.
And, while the bay just beside it
heaved between free fluid and gelled
clots of weed, the street was still,
and had long dreams of being a bride.
Down below the last stratum in its
corridor of ice, back flat against the
grit, hands folded in its lap, it was
as white as absence is, white as
unsuspected feeling, white as old
regret.

The pier suffered this year, too,
I'm told; lost footage. Its
outermost pilings twisted up; some

bent. The gray boardwalk went with
it to a point, but then knelt down on one
knee and stooped into the bay
like a heavy paper fan—or like some beast
that tumbled in to drink at one end
in order to save its far-off other.
So the wood road went, at last,
where it always teased it would
and I can only imagine
the pilgrim-tourists still faithful
to the walk, going out, tipping off
its brink, gathering like red and white coral
in the shoal water below.

The winter that I lived there also had
its acts of small ruination. Two good
cripplings, I remember: a transom
ripped out of the inn, and a man found
in the dunes, half-frozen, whispering
that he'd lost his fingers looking
for God. He did lose two, from frostbite;
the others remained warm, though of
little use afterwards. All winter
whole plates of ice accrued on the
windward sides of the houses,
throwing their balances further off-center.
Sleet pelted and gathered
with great constancy, making window
reefs, closing the throats of locks,
sealing off age lines in the architecture
where shrill drafts slithered in
and licked the children on the floor;
when they cried from it, much of their
voices was taken off by the wind.

That's really all we ever heard, except
for the buoy bells. And those we really
didn't know we heard, they were so
familiar: the thin-voiced one and
the one that spoke like a clay pot.
But between them and the constant
gale, they beat everything else mute:
a wind, a deep thud and a chime,
sometimes striking together, more
often not; a constant presence in
the chest that made you think there
was an unseen heart out there somewhere on the point, one like your
own, uncertain and dull from the
daily certainty of facing deep water
for no reason that was clear or
good enough.

It was a strange town then; it's a
strange town now, borrowed for the
weekend by neighbors who drive
three hours out to sea to meet and bed
each other. The rest of the time, in
winter, anyway, it's left to even
stranger souls: inbred fishers, some
society involved in properties, some
hard-lidded boys only breathing for
the drugs and incest a small island
has to offer, souls altogether that
lack prophecy, do no moon-reading with
a wrist in the tide, have no sense of
quick loss. The only social law on the
peninsula, at last, is endurance and
erosion, and maybe the shrill business

of pretense. And yet beneath all,
it is what it's always been. We are
what we were born to be: soft shell-
less things on difficult rock with a
sea tearing chunks out of the neck
of a storm; mindless creatures
staring up at mindless elements,
with some terrible few seeking a
sad stone in the center of another
eye.

And though the nest of timbers
and gables that was the town
had too many widows of too many sorts,
still, sometimes there were days,
I remember, most of them near spring,
when you could swear the seaweed
had bloomed. And though the town
still seemed brittle, sitting on itself
beside the bay, you could catch
a cool drift stumbling through the world
that said: there is benign affection
between men—some passageway
between the season that tears us
and the season that plants those
pieces of us in the wet earth and bids
them come up again whole. And on
such days, when out of circumstance
and deprivation, you find yourself
licking salt off a stranger's red throat,
minutely kissing small, unseen hairs,
the tight folds where a muscle tucks,
a bone sockets, you know gradually
that you're meant for the deepest sort

of flesh, for the room in the heart no
one enters without removing the hands.

All day the feeling's with you.
You echo in the bed, trying not to name
it as a creature of any element,
but something is there that's godly.
Something's been a thread, gathering
the orphans you've been harboring
in your life. Something makes the town
a home for some part of you.

By nightfall, in the room above the bay,
you are altered. You burn candles
that you set in saucers of still water,
in case you chance to fall asleep.
Outside, of course, the wind-bitch
cuts a tooth on the glass; the flames
altogether wobble. You count their
eyes in everything that reflects.
You sense yourself as a sort of soft
fire, too, a tongue of it, mouthed
and rounded into a vowel that flickers
with rarity. You think of the eye.
You sleep.
At daybreak of the next day,
there are hard lids of wax
hanging on the saucer's waters
where the candles have guttered to their nubs
and drunk. There is the street, the sea,
the tiny and remnant lives, the sudden
conviction that the stranger
you kept out of the wind yesternight,
though nameless, could be as much

the reason for your life as you
yourself could be. You're silent
in the cold, bright room.

As the panes begin to knock in the
morning wind, you want to waken,
to rise, to visit the distant point,
to speak with the twin and deaf bells
there that stare out, away from the
harbor, away from the town.

A Soldier Dreams

Mildew in the seams and left
in patterns where the pants have wrinkled
on the body: he is sleeping
under green above below
beside around green forever growing
haltless and moist.
                    War—
the morning hot.
And not-awake he says, *This* is what
love is. When it is too
stiff-cocked, young and wet,
too long-driven and deafening itself,
till coming and not's like a blur,
like any feeling is when felt in one way
on one nerve, each slice of the day,
by the ten fingers pressing there,
a mouth and a hard body made of hair,
breathing moisture in the cup
of that ear. Yes, it is wet-loving,
everywhere and too much,
with no time to be alone, to remember
one's own country,
to have a shore and stand on it,

singing across glinting water, *I love him,*
my whole body inside the lousy
khaki loves him.

Dawn

already hot from the night before.
Asleep: snakes mate. The sun's rising
is more through steam than mist.
It's the wet-numb,
the dumb longing after longing,
the eye-opened hole in sleep
that the yellow bastards know so well,
the rice boys and little buddha-men
who steal about
like angels, putting candies
between our legs, who giggle and are gone.
And we, the six of us, sleep the last
few seconds back to the nothing
and the blast.
And I remember, yes, remember
the man I love all clearly now,
oh yes, him again
somewhere straight on through the other side
of the thick earth,
him and me Stateside and under
the acres of sweat, time, the talking
of sweet-dirt, the ruin of sheets.
We're present and accounted, him and me,
sliding down the bridge of dreams
on oil and petroleum jellies,
until, my God,
we're just like angels,
air in our bodies and cocks
and souls all pumped with white-fire:
this, it's this.

This under the wet and waiting,
the betrayal by children,
the mob at home dividing eggs,
this when the three grenades awake
and not one of our six
hears the other five die.
This the love of the flesh,
the great spirit in our grease
and bile and pulps
and cream, and those our pumping parts
and ports of entry,
our bones, and in the footage
wound forever up in two, three, six
mens' guts:
the love, the air, yes God,
forgiveness and more, Kenny, more.

Crazyboy Wisechild

Crazyboy's brain had a wound on its left;
had a thumbprint, a lie, a polka-dot tit
made purple by accident. It could
have been his newborn eye that got put out
as easily, or his nose that was mashed
into pigs, but no,
the doctor's thumb had crushed the brain-flower
instead, left a clam-shaped thing bleeding,
which sponged, rose. Soon there was a tuck,
a thoughtlost, one blue coin, a blotched
crab hiding under brain-shelf, waiting.
Crazyboy walked pitched to the left.
Crazyboy forgot his right foot often.
Crazyboy spoke to the fate-bird,
tongue slabbed into suet—yes, he,
Crazy-He, who lived by the dam,
who sang:
Loo la   loo loo
without voice   to trees
without seasons.

Crazyboy first saw Wisechild as gas.
The Wisechild said: No no come back when I'm done.

Crazyboy cried and went to watch fish three days,
to watch thimbles, put bees in bottles
after they'd stung three days.
He saw Wisechild again; Wisechild had shape.
He glowed like a lampshade.
Crazyboy could see his white bones through
his white skin.
Wisechild talked inside Crazyboy's head:
Hello, said Wisechild, Hello.
Hello, said Crazyboy, Hello.
How many fingers have you? Wisechild asked.
Crazyboy showed him.
Is that *all*? Wisechild said. And Crazyboy cried
and ran, tipped, down the wall of the dam
to the gravel pit.
Don't cry, said Wisechild at the end of the wall,
at the pit, in between the gray kernels of stone,
I'll show you a trick. Look. Look, there
on your feet, *there's* more. Two more by five more!
Crazyboy laughed to the left; didn't cry.
Wisechild said: Ah, this means, you know,
you'll never die.

When Crazyboy was two he ate the glass.
When Crazyboy was six he wished to wear fire.
When Crazyboy was eight he painted milk.
When Crazyboy was ten he wore a glove on his tongue.
When Crazyboy was eighteen
he got bit on the penis by a dog.
When Crazyboy was thirty he carried a book.
At thirty-six, Crazyboy saw Wisechild as a gas.
Wisechild guttered like a hissing flame,
wavering in and out. He was a curtain,
a picture on the water. Coldfire was Wisechild,

wobbling his silence in the dark green pine nook,
that little room, the one left without furniture
in the needle trees; that one
with the little smoke hole for light to tip in
like a wand, a spill, a flume; to tip in
clear and viscid, to pour on Wisechild's flame,
the flame shuddering with a chill—it
goes in and out.
All the small inchless needles,
both the red-brown and the black-green
are seeable and seen, countable and numbered
in the mind of God, which lives for eons,
mindless, thumping eons,
choked up with days and lives,
that unending knot of leaves glutting
a bankless brook; the mind of God which lives
for this white instant when Wisechild comes
to burn up the woods with gases.
Hello, said Wisechild, Hello.
Hello, said Crazyboy, Hello.

Once Wisechild said to Crazyboy:
Play with *this*: why are leaves like fish?
Crazyboy cried; he ran.
His legs went up and down the dam.
Behind, the Moon asked him: *Why?*
Under him, the gravel stones squeaked; they mocked.
He didn't know. He didn't *know*.
The heart in his rib-house beat its head
against the bars; it rose to the smoke hole;
pecked its beak at the inside hollow
of his throat: he didn't know!
Six days running he had to swallow the heart
and talk it down, talk it down with sweets

and threats of the dog who'd bit his penis.
It was Wisechild who talked from inside the
heart-bird: Why are leaves like fish?
Crazyboy knelt for hours at the gravel pit
spitting and spitting, hawking his lungs
and throat. But the talk stayed in and he
couldn't cough up the heart nor keep it still:
Leaves and fish   leaves and toes.

He stood at the spillway, crying, throwing
tears down into the flow below.
On the other side, a ring of yellow leaves
was turning on the water's top,
swimming head after tail, waiting to be fed.
And he saw them inside his brain.
He ran to the other side, the still side of the dam.
He saw them spinning, feeding on light
and he knew, he *knew*.
He spun like they did on the dam:
Look—this is how! he said: There, *this* is!
Wisechild laughed: You must be hungry, he said,
Here eat this.
And he reached into his rib-house and took out
his white heart: it was like the moon,
like the moon on the water's top at night.
There were leaves turning inside it.
It went down Crazyboy's throat and inside.
He got frightened and trembled
and then all of space was in him
and time turned its many spirals in him
and he felt his teeth in the dog's penis
and his face full of milk from the sun and moon
that opened like a jewelweed inside his head.
Oh, said Crazyboy, I'll never die.

Look, I'll never die. Look.
What do you see? asked Wisechild.
The wind went away and the light in Crazyboy's
body went up the smoke hole.
I see a red clam in my head, said Crazyboy.
The trees wavered like gas, too.
Ah, said Wisechild, ah. Here, slowly
Child, all slowly open the bone.
I shall, at last, touch it.

The Beekeeper's Sister

for Jane

On a good day, she walked well enough,
but there were times when she walked with
her legs nearly backwards—thin dogs,
someone called them, strays whose noses
had wandered to points other than the one
her eye steered toward. And when they
strayed too far apart and pitched her over,
she walked with her hands, like a hooped-
over creature, an always-hissing cat
with a harp in its spine. They were strange,
her hands, closed like a great pair of buds,
turned into fat spits. She held them as if
she were always pulling a wet thread
through her uneven fingers.

They said she'd live, as best she could,
until she was 14 or 12 or 15 and then,
quite relentlessly, she'd pass away,
while those who had watched for the
near-dozen years, as she walked on all
fours and ate yellow capsules of jelly,
were forced again to witness helplessly
and survive it.

At moments through the years,
each of these witnesses would
admit secretly—but never to anyone else,
certainly not to each other—that her
crippled stumping down the hallways,
the flailing table times—even the
terrible last evening when she could
not be kept in bed, but stuttered through
each of the rooms in a last orbit—
that all this, all of it, was possessed
of a strange and awful loveliness; that
all of life, and perhaps every life,
was laced with this same thin, red beauty
also.

        Each would come to sense something
in her old lying behind the sofa,
narrating the fringes, the machine-work,
the wood flutings. A gathering significance
came with remembering her falls
into reverie. When wakened by a branch
at the window, they would each watch
the memory of her circuits through the house
again, arms out, touching everything
as if to name it, and each would sense
the passage, through time, of a creature,
one of the countless such that inch, like
water-worms, through the world, beneath
the fast plateaus of fact. An angel, they'd
say, the visitation in their lives of an
angel of some purpose. And each would
almost believe *this is the reason for
death*: to give our old facts time enough
to waken from their callousness, to grow
luminous as gas; to fast fall apart

and reveal their small ghost of sense.

There was a brother. He saw something
of this in her long before the others did;
saw it in himself, too. And he tried to show
his sister the mote in her own eye,
like a mute pointing out a window.
But she entirely failed to see him; never
heard him, in fact. Sometimes she sat
mercilessly in his place at table; almost
daily asked her mother, in her thick
nose-voice, Who's he? Who's he?
After ten years of it, the boy made a game
of it; made up names, occupations:
I'm the fish licenser, he'd tell her,
I've come for the loose lettuce leaves;
I'm renting a room in the garret while I
go to veterinary college, young lady;
I'll treat your elephants with colds,
your toothaches in mastodons, your
mal à la gorge in giraffes.
　　　　　　　　He'd look
at her critically through his fork; for
a moment he thought she'd cleared,
seen him. She looked uncritically at the
wall behind his face instead; never let
on whether she'd heard or not; seemed
instead to forget whatever was his
question; she counted the salt she'd
spilled on the tablecloth. The brother
bit his lip, stared at her, went to
school. She counted until the sun fell
onto the salt. Then she thought she'd
count the sun, too, but couldn't think

how; tried to scoop it up, lick it off her
hands. Nothing, nothing, her nose-
voice said in the kitchen, to mother in
the back cupboard. She went to the
window and bit at it. Nothing! Nothing!
Nothing! she snorted, until she'd put
the saltshaker through the pane of glass:
then it was quiet, utterly, like the inside
of a jar. And the sun was spreading on
her flat face like sense.

Once the brother fell ill, no one could
say why. He left his studies and, though
it was spring, kept to his dim room in
the head of the house. He was heard
to pray; or thought to weep. They forbade
the sister to go there, praying aside
that it sunk in, but she never had gone
there before, so when she didn't hear
them or forgot what they'd said, it didn't
matter. And, not seeing him, she no
longer asked who he was at table: he
had vanished without ever having been.
Instead, there were spring
trees and the lawn. There were bees
that looked like the beads in Mother's
drawer. All day they walked around
inside the apple flowers, counting and
counting the hairs, while lard-shaped
clouds went by overhead and juicy
creatures came out of the dirt to be
swallowed by birds. She narrated the
lawn, the weather: this may have taken
weeks. Nothing was clear.

Except

that something odd called to her every
other day—something first in the
branches. Then in the loamy dirt.
She'd turn to it every time; stare at the
vacant place: nothing, there was nothing.
Then the bees began to leave the stiff
petals and to settle on her whenever she
slept. She dreamed they came to her,
one and one, until they were thick upon
her. She dreamed they drank from her,
with the aid of their many quick feet.
They drank her dream of them; they drank
her early death. Her sleep. She dreamed
they'd come, like sponges, to drink
whatever pain they could. That was it:
to drink pain! Then everything was
very clear. Eyes open, she stared up
at the branches and the soft perfumes.
She blinked. The bees came to drink
pain, they drank pain. A long slab of
cloud blundered into the house. And she
knew there was a boy in their attic; that
his face was like glass; that his eyes
once sought hers; that they no longer
tried to seek anyone; that he loved
another boy; that this frailty made him
rattle like a pea in his own ear; that it
was in him that the bees had nested;
that it was his heart in which they left
their sick honey; that he, poor boy,
was her only brother.

She was running. She pounded through

the first floor hall, hot as an engine;
threw her feet up the stairs, as if they
were shovels of dirt. She was pursued;
she was drawn. She clawed at the
floral sprays on the wallpaper.
You, you, she hooted.
She climbed the steps heaving.
It was urgent, an insect timed by the
moon; she knew her moment would be
brief and then the cloud would have
passed, the gray soup in her head would
have come back: she'd forget.
She barked at his white door, battered
against it with the back of her arms,
her neck. She rammed her bundled hands
at the violet glass knob until it turned.
The door opened. He was at the gable
window. There were cloths, sheets.
There were half-glasses of water. A tray.

His eyes were the color of plums.
From the exertion, she had lost control
of her spine, and when she tried to walk
to him, she could only throw herself
on the floor. Then he was kneeling
over her and she pulled herself up by
his robe. She caught a knee, climbed
his body as painfully as a fish would
climb. You, she breathed in the back
of her nose. Then she pitched forward,
her mouth dribbling against his chest,
smearing the camphor jelly. There was
no air. She was turning dark.
Then her eyes were even with his and

he was carrying her to the window.
It's all right, all right, he was saying.
But his voice was hollow, used up:
Who would guarantee his promises to
anyone? it said.
            The body of the
cloud was passing over into the next
street. She was chewing her teeth.
I *know* you, she told his chest.
Yes, all right, he said, all right. She
was dim. I *know* you, she whispered.
She saw the half-glass of water on
the night table again. Then she fell
asleep. Once or twice she said:
Beekeeper, beekeeper, while the boy
held her, white-faced, ashen,
wondering who or what, in a life,
knew anything, anyone.

A Place in the Family

It's odd to remember that first: the ice,
all lighted up in its odd way,
probably just by the moon and the torchlight
on shore; but maybe even lighted up
in its own right, too.
I sometimes think that maybe water,
when it goes to ice, gives up its heat
to give off light instead; or maybe
it's just in remembering that things do this.
And *this*: all around, the light-water
was enclosed by the dark, as if in a big room,
a church hall. And this seemed—
well, I don't know—it seemed like
it was not just darkness,
but a kind of space
where silent animals lined the walls.
It had a thickness to it, like water,
a denseness maybe, like mud.
I want very much to say it was
like *waiting*.

I don't remember the breakthrough
or any impact—no shock, certainly.

I just suddenly saw that the whole lake
had been silently broken into a wheel,
and that the great cracks
that had appeared everywhere
all pointed at me. Pieces sank from this,
like pie slices. I, too, sank. Then silence—
I remember the silence most clearly.
And things thrown at my face: slivers
of mirror, plates, rock. I thought:
the hull of the earth's blown all open
and it's Jesus-day; me with no intentions
to talk of, no deeds, even my personal
death blurred over with the end of
all Christians via holocaust; nothing
mine to show for, to wear, to give away
or buy me passage.

And the next I knew was them, pulling
the hands out from under the armpits
and talking me down, unbending
the arms which they pushed halfway
deep into a heap of dung
that lay steaming on the floor.
There were six—no, five; or—
no, I can't say. They were just lights
and shadows overlaid, shifting.
Just breath hot on the block of numbness
I'd abandoned to them.
There was a woman with a limp, I know;
and a dark one who I knew hated me.
With one the thought that I must
be naked was comfortable; with the other,
terrible—the red hair between my legs
felt like a wound when she was there.

At times there was tea with whiskey,
I think,
though it could have been
heart's blood and livers for all I knew.
I drank it too hot; sank; prayed:
please God, don't let me break apart;
and if I do, don't let my pieces scatter;
don't let fish eat my parts;
don't let some be recovered while others
be lost;
and don't let no one put together
the partial body nor the partial eye
and stand me up with gaps and losses.
Oh God, don't let no one
save me this way.

For days they fed me broth—the five or
seven of them—and for days, I don't know
why, but I thought it was poison
they were giving me. It may have been
fever; it seems mad now,
but I was taken with the notion then,
in part at least, and was too weary
to protest or say it outright.
So I ate the drink, chewed it like fat;
felt it was the meat of death
they'd slipped like slivered nuts
into the soup. And I *died*, you see.
Yes, I believe I did die, in some way
outside the issue of the fever and the brain
nearly at a boil. I died, daily and in stages,
but steadily, surrendering with colicky
resentment and a dull vague gratitude,
until I was no more the plank of ice

hung between the nourishment
and the poison.
And here, like a winter fish,
I dreamed: I was under the ice again,
looking up through it at the sky,
at things living overhead,
wonderful and distorted by the surface.
Sometimes I surfaced and looked up;
there was nothing overhead.
Only the reflection of what was below.
Oh, and I can't say what was
the feeling at seeing that the sky was
empty. And I can't say
what it felt like to see the business
and riches of the lake that continued
forever downward.
All I knew was I had a dim place
in the family,
and that it steered the dim life
that was asleep in me.
It was the stone anchor,
I the red creature who let its hair
loosen on the tide.

Owl

An owl shattered the windshield of Clare's mother's car,
broke the glass into squarish teeth.
She lost control of the vehicle; it skidded, slid sidelong
off the road, halfway into a shallow brook—
all this so quickly that it seemed to happen twice,
then again, then to jolt suddenly into full stop,
an evening snow falling quietly through the hollow
web of glass, on which snow-light caught, broke.
Only the dog barking in the back seat seemed
to occur in full time.
She had barely seen it—a clipped moment
of the animal's panic perhaps; mostly
the opened feathers as they appeared
in her headlights, the large shadow coming
close before her face; then the sound of breakage,
the pained *Coo* in the bird's throat,
the rain of cubes blowing in;
at last, the wing-spread impact
of the bird flung open on her breasts.
In the stillness, she stared out the window
at the new and remarkable snow.
A square of glass fell in, then nothing.
The dog was far away.

Clare wrote to her mother, *You wonder what*
it's like here, who I am as a result of this place?
A curiosity, at best; just as large a thumb
in Delhi as I was amid the good china
and relatives in Connecticut.
I'm a holiday niece here too, always
that third of a trio of similar cousins
whose name gets lost in introductions.
But no,
it's not a question of What, or even of Who
I am, my dear (that's old, and at times so am I).
The question maddeningly put is simply Where?
Where am I, at last? This is the issue of Place,
position.

Clare's mother stared through the broken window.
The air that came at her was cold, of course,
just below freezing.
In the sudden quiet following the accident,
she could hear the thin brook running
under its thin skin of ice,
licking away at its own underside.
She thought of the car wheels having broken
this open, of them sitting now in the brook water
while it iced over again, surrounding the
rounds of rubber.
She wondered if she still had her glasses on.
Two hours passed. Three.

Clare wrote to her mother, *India,*
that great coral reef, what it hasn't itself
accrued, it has enveloped.
Yes, Mother, of course, I feel at times

that these are badly borrowed robes,
borrowed landscapes; that my time here
is merely the ungraceful fall of another
white woman gone spiritually native.
Nevertheless, I feel a task for me, don't you?
Feel it as clearly as one would
a bolt of good cloth. Ah, the lust
for assimilation? To wear the silk and weave
of India as easily as one wears one's
utter nude? To be an ebbing foreigner,
fingering these yellow places until one's
flesh is saffron flesh: to be what one sees?
Think of it, Mother, to see it and also to be it.
That's the conscious dilemma, isn't it?
And isn't this my task? At least,
my long-standing and isolate metaphor?
Is it a way home?
Helen suggested that. And I thought, Do we,
all of us here, do we tease from this
cluttered country the ghost of our own?
And in a bent and backward way do we try
to be the creature born to a Yankee time
and pinpoint place by being a creature lodged
in someone else's? I think that would be
task enough.
I also think lately that it is a way
of learning the basic comedy, the one
that tells us no one is a special flesh in any
special place; it's all just ribbons tacked to clocks
—the news, Mother, that we each house
only a special ghost who never knows
foot-on-earth, never sees the telling of the time,
never comes to names—this also
is task, a business beyond mere foreignness,

Mother, don't you think?

The dog leaped back and forth, mad, trapped,
clawing the side windows, then stumbled
over the front seat and through the crumpled
space in the door. He ran, barking,
circling the car endlessly, first in one direction
then the other.
Everything came at him. He jumped away
from the twicks of the cooling engine,
sprang up at what was underfoot, muddied
the brook a hundred times with running away
from it, running back through it.
He snapped at trees, at the water; he was most
afraid of the car, lying like a great egg
on a side.
Still, there was the woman inside staring
placidly through the shattered windshield.
He didn't run off. Instead,
with false starts and sprintings away,
with yelping, he sniffed his way back,
whimpered, called her—at last, nosed
her coat. She was still.
After a long while, he climbed into the back seat,
whining, shaking with the cold.
At last, he fell silent.

Clare wrote to her mother, *I often think I
am not entirely of this world.
No, that's simply it: I inhabit a loneliness
instead, one such that comes of
falling alone for years down one's own well,
there unearthing unexpectedly
the under-river passage that opens on*

the wells of others. Yes, the aloneness
that reaches those others at a place
beyond themselves . . .
It's night here now; been raining for weeks.
And I inhabit an eye;
live the life of an odd eye,
which sees beyond the scheme of light
and dark into lightlessness; one which can
name the blurred and darkened kin
who dwell there.
I live the life of the eye
of a mole, coursing through
loose mud . . .

A dry snow covered the hood.
This melted with the remnant heat of the
engine, but held itself in place
as a slush.
Steam rose from it; in part, it froze.
Clare's mother gradually surrendered to shock.
The poor owl bled, twitched softly, also shocked,
while outside a strange whiteness revealed itself
and hid itself, became nearly a thing
and not a thing, became an entity
and an absence, a coolness in the dark
or a white fact, a fact in an utterness,
one nearly awake, but truly not awake.
Unknowingly, Clare's mother reached
to the dashboard, pressed a metal knob;
the headlights, buried in snow,
went out.

Clare wrote to her mother, *When I flew*
to India, it was also night. I arrived

before dawn. The sky below at the line
was a mix of peach colors and old blood.
Thin charcoal clouds pulled through this
like a weave.
The rest of the air was cold blue.
The city was still in darkness, distinguished
in part by its many small lights.
Nevertheless, the effect was of its slumber.
I slowly felt that only I was awake on the plane.
Not the pilot. Nor the other travelers.
Only me. There was not even a clear sense
that there was a plane
or that I was moving with it; just
the wakefulness existed.
This frightened me, as everything after and
before has frightened me,
frightened and slaughtered some private quarter
in the heart.
I so longed for comfort—but, my dear,
who was there, thinking or heart-beating
in the whole world but me?
Could I beg my own comfort? Could I give it?
This was the eye.
I watched this eye land with the steady weight
of a planet visiting whatever orb is kindred
but greater,
this while the horizon reddened
and the hot dry day built its spiral.

It grew colder.
The snow turned grainy and then ceased.
The brook halted. Half-light gathered
into some things, abandoned others.
The owl tried to move itself, but, its wing bones

broken, it failed.
The water was voiceless. There was
nothing there but the small pain,
the closed field around it; no other thing
in the field,
no brown bird, no earth under it;
only a tossed bramble of hay and winterweed
floating like an island,
bearing a candle-point of fire.
And that fire was the pain.
There was no sky there. Nor was there one
elsewhere.
Clare's mother noticed that a great glinting
wheel had somehow opened in her windshield
and that she was in her car, not in bed;
and that she was gently petting
the pelt of a bird
that lay splayed open on her chest; in fact,
that she was weeping, repeating the words,
Poor dear, poor dear.
She was surprised to feel herself filled
with a deep sadness.
She wondered how she came to wear this long
coarse robe of snow and wings.

Easter Crossing

3:1

I write as the shore goes down
over the horizon. It is March, late night.
Below are my charges, my flock, men
and families whose priest I am. We sail
for the Americas. The land of our fathers
is dead with famine and despair. We flee
and yet do not flee—
the hand of God is hard to read,
at best. What He requires baffles,
angers me.

3:2

Seabirds hover; I dreamt
that fish circled also under the ship—
this like form and its perfect shadow.

3:3

John Fay has the fever. He raves
all night of home, green hills and soup.
There's a terrible poetry in him
when he does this—and his face,
a sweet, dappled face, like a calf's,
is blissful as it burns and pours out sweat.
Father, he says to me,
I see America and it's all golden;
then he wants to confess, but I know
there's no sin in him.
I feed him the oranges and limes I sold
my father's watch to buy
before we set sail. He will live,
I feel.

3:4

> "The last enemy that shall be destroyed
> is death."
>
> (1 CORINTHIANS 15:26)

The Dougherty baby died today;
the mother will tomorrow or perhaps
next day. We have had
a Burial at Sea: I'd never seen
such a thing before. The father
is a small man, nearly a boy;
he wept in my arms shamelessly
as we stood on the deck . . .

No matter what arrangement I make

with myself regarding practicality
and the absolute facts of rot and death,
I cannot, no I cannot, imagine
our dropping the babe into the sea . . .

3 : 5

St. Paul speaks of the Priesthood
of Suffering—a damaged man, but
there's truth in him—he does not
mean mere acceptance of suffering.
And if he does, I do not; that is
mere complacency and defeat by ordinary
fear. To take on his priesthood
is to take on not fear, but *terror*:
to find the suffering beneath
what it's said to be and not be.
It's folly to think it is a goodness
to feel famine or to die of it;
nor is it a goodness to stave off
pleasure with a cross.
Pleasure-taking does not pertain.
Do what pleasure you will;
it is not relevant to this.
The suffering is not and never was
the *shadow* of pleasure, nor its overthrow.
It is the desire before and after pleasure
for the unknowable;
and it is only for the few,
only one at a time.

3:6

I feel today that I have no faith,
only stubbornness, habits . . .

3:7-8

There is a storm upon us; nothing
is as it was; there is no world, no time
or place. It seems that there was
always only this. Since yesterday,
we have been forbidden the deck.
A crewman fell onto his back,
his spine ruined.
The day and night are indistinguishable.
I've been below with the families.
We can only sit or lie flat;
to stand is to break a bone.
One cannot fear for one's self,
lest this make the others' fears
grow and consume all. No one's slept.
To fetch my stole for confession
I had to crawl up the deck
to my cabin; it was flooded,
my papers sodden. Oddly, I wept for this.
I sat on the floor in the brackish water,
aware only of my feet shrinking
in my shoes. I cried out,
I want to live! I *choose* to live!
while the storm howled as deaf as God
outside, above, within.

3:9

I cannot write today.

3:10

In the wind
is an emptiness,
a pocket of stillness.

3:11

I've read that men driven to despair
with God's silence will pray to Hell
and, for this, they are damned.
I understand such recourse to darkness,
but not damnation, no. If only
because it is not coin nor wives, nor
is it land for which these damned pray—
that's just a cruel notion. No,
they truly ask for a *voice*, a red
meat-flayed voice with any answer
or no answer, but only that there be
a voice, a presence.
And to some, Hell makes answer.
And if it is so that these souls are damned,
it is in *this* way: to be taken
from the flat world; sent to sea,
to sand, to peaks which no one knows,
no one sees, possessed by a faith

in an instinct that lies past
the wreck of God and the heart;
to be a voice oneself, without a tongue.
Or a tongue without a red word. Or
to be both. Or
to be alone with both.

3:12

Mary Haddon sold fish at Galway.
She talks much of the fish that must
be beneath us and everywhere in the sea.
Sometimes she sings her hawking songs.
In good weather she's up with the sailors,
hauling a net like any man,
laughing at the flipping silver
she's pulled out of the sea; a good-hearted
woman, a great favorite with the men,
and every girl's sister in sorrow.
I ask her often to remember me
in her prayers.

3:13

When I was a boy, of course, I served
the altar, but was, they told me,
given to visions. Partly nonsense, I'm sure,
but, in part, real visitation
and longing beyond flesh, needs
clothed in things borrowed from a church

which was threadbare.
My dreams became not my own.
I was sent to the priest
who told me to be wary of the Devil in this,
as he dwelt in such Fancy. Dreams,
he said, were the first steps toward loss
of soul, madness.
Soon I was taken into the church
and taught the faith.
It was a faith, I know, made of fear;
built to confound and addle away
rich impulse, rich doubt.
It rose like a monolith through youth.
It fell. And when it fell,
there was neither fear nor impulse left,
only destitution.
I comforted a flock, but not myself;
responsible for souls with more faith
than I.
And what out of this? *Doubt.*
Something always doubts.
Through doubt, I've come to see *within* things,
to peel a word, a truth,
a man's soul into division; to name
the parts and counties that,
through flux and aggregation,
have remained lost in each other
and untitled. This is my gift: a loss
of heart, a facile mind, passions
as hot and obscure as ice—and doubt,
honed like a surgeon's knife.

In ten days it will be Easter . . .

3:14

I write now with a dead hand.
Two hours since, young Dougherty
came to me and stood in the doorway.
He said, *Father, I've something*
to give you—no, no, be still—it's
only words. Then he was still. He held
onto the low rafters while the ship rolled.
I know your heart, you see;
and I know you have shards and notions there
none of us'll ever dream of. I know
it's terrible, Father, and I know that
I will make it all the more grievous tonight.
But, list, Father, listen; if only
you saw yourself as I see you,
a man so good and fine it brings tears
to the eyes, a man whose gravest
errors are beautiful to witness.
If only you had my eyes, Father. I would
give you them . . .
Then he seemed altered, perhaps lightened;
said, *Remember what I tell you, now. Forgive me.*

And he went onto the deck, chose not
to pray; instead spit at the moon.
And then gently he let himself over the side
of the ship into God knows what acre
of the sea and into what deep hour of the night.

I am the only soul who knows this.
I sit with this knowledge, with this,

his terrible gift.
... Lord God,
I am only a man, only a man ...

3:15

3:16

3:17

3:18

The lamp, swinging,
nearly outing itself.
Shadow pours from corner to corner
to corner. I, too, spill—
from compassion to comprehension
to rage.
Where is the realm wherein these unite?
Within, within ...

3:19

Pain and suffering are *not* the same thing.

3:20

We are strong, in our way.
But only in our way.

3:21

Mary came to me at night; had, she said,
something to say. She sat at my small table,
chewing her lip.
Father, she said, her face flushed and ruddy
as a man's, *we can put out the nets,*
you know, and make a drag, see. She wove
her fingers to show me. *God knows what*
the currents do down there; there's
a chance we'd find him.
I said nothing.
She knew as well as I it was foolish;
that we'd also only have to drop him
into the sea again, the only alteration
being the rites and the widow's horror
renewed.
The notion withered.
She stared at the table, then at me
for a long time, reading my thoughts perhaps,

or beyond my thoughts.
We sat together. I came to understand that
she was much like my poor sister; that there
is sometimes a bond for one's other half
and that it will leap the very world
if need be.
Ah, a man's body, Father, she said sadly,
there's more to it than just blood
and bleeding.

3:22

SERMON FOR EASTER SERVICE: TEXT: JAMES 1:15
(God forbid I ever speak it)

Kiss Death! Whine like the Jew, my brethren!
Howl like Greeks! We've given all,
even History. Cut cord and let
whatever gift and small treasure (a coin,
a pin, a gold tooth to grin with),
slide from our face.
Nothing's left! We are nothing
but Death itself, incarnating.
And today is the birth of its Spider!
I say: Death is even greater than itself!
It is hunger; it is endurance.
It is resident in our prevailing young,
while we all thank God
and go on walking with skull
and with bone forever:
it is our life! We are a species

of death-smelling mice.
Death is our familiar; he comes
with the post.
And he is not mere corruption,
dissolution nor fear, but utter Loss rather,
perpetuating Loss
of the sort that is without end.
I say: without end!
Had it an end, we'd have long since
raised a Celtic plinth; cut a cross
and then, Children, turned the gory absence
to the balming of, say, Spring.
But no, we have climbed into
the jellied wound and nested!
Our Spring only flowers the same
dark root we find intricated everywhere
in our ribs,
the same claw tenanted in dream.
I say: it is not *stoppage, this our Death,*
not cessation, but eternal Winter
followed by the unwrap of a sooty Spring,
a green-seeming flower, but
a black one in truth, reaching back up
into our history. It is a gaining *Death!*
It is in our hearts and in our eyes!
We speak it! And eat it! And bless it!
Say what you will;
tell me it's fair and shares the bed
with the rose; tell me
there's the Resurrection of the Body—
I say: there is still *the face of Death!*
And that his kingdom, staring out of our eyes,
is vaster than hope.
He searches ever out another acre

in us to spawn upon.
I say: you are his engine, you who
make children and pass his sour tongue along!
I say: ours is a generating Death!
A crime so old it has come to make sense.

He takes from us; we nod.
He leaves his terrible loveliness,
a body afloat, bereft of blood . . .

3:23

Confessions all evening.
John Fay walking again.
I take a passage out of Paul; will speak
my sermon on Faith.
A boy asks me, *What did Jesus do*
while He was dead? He asks
everyone, his sister beside him.
Three birds above for hours.
The air thin. Cool.

3:24—Easter Morning

> "But now is Christ risen from the dead,
> and become the first fruits of them that slept."
> (1 CORINTHIANS 15:20)

The weather was good: thick heads of cloud,
clear sun, blue heavens and sea. Passage
overhead, below, between.

I said the Mass on deck where it was
greatly windy.

I don't remember where or when it veered
the other way. Nothing else changed.
The weather held, as did the good wind.
My parish stood; they'd eaten the meager meal
of wafers. They stood facing me;
I them.
Sailors hung in knots around our circle,
devout in their own way, but still sailors
before they were Believers or Countrymen.
Each cloud passed over as firm
and unaltered as a continent
sliding across the map of the visible world.

And somewhere in the constant flux,
young Dougherty's body, fresh in the icy waters,
undid itself from the underparts
of the ship, and rose to the surface
where we made an Easter effort
to treat of God's reasons and Pain.
The widow collapsed, vomited.
Mary held her in her arms; stared at
the bloated corpse, then me.

I don't know what I felt . . . I cannot say
what I felt . . .

3:25

3:26

3:27

Confiteor Deo . . .
Lord God, listen now, if ever
You did resemble the human heart.
I am in pain and confess the secret dream
that has risen ceaselessly in my mind,
at night, awake, asleep, always the same:
thin light, falling through water or time
upon the pale glow of his flesh
as it drifts up, serene in absolute
and boundless space.
There is a pearl in his mouth,
the face smiles through the depthless fathoms.
He has always been rising, climbing
the stairs of fish and salt to me—
my God, the boy makes a gift of his death!—
his perfect and eternal body,
the icy, weeping face, his voice and blessings,
his dead frail beauty, his infinite regard.

Please forgive me, my God;
I have striven to forgive You.

3:28

There is a feeling of vastness
to the sea today and to the sky overhead.

I feel I have never known so clearly
that beyond ourselves is, in fact, the world—
a vast world beyond any thought
we can have of it.
There is a feeling of huge indifference to it.
I believe today that this is what is Holy.

3:29

The *"readiness to receive."* Reading Paul
this comes to me: it
is always through emptying
that we receive.
Through a lapse, through utter loss,
through a rent in the fabric of the mind.

3:30

He hovers, more spirit
than dream.

We've had the second burial by water—
not today, several days back—
his sack weighted with sand.
Few watched the service.
I saw thin ice on the folds of the canvas;
imagined it gaining on the boy within—
between the red lashes,
the slight hairs upon his upper lip.
His lips would be blue . . .

He hangs
the flesh of flesh,
the spirit of flesh.

3 : 31

This is the middle of the sea, Mary
told me. *On either hand there's equal water,*
she said.

What did Jesus do?
she says to the boy
with the sister and the single question.
Why, He went swimming, *child,*
wouldn't you?

4 : 1

> "Brethren, I write no new commandment unto you,
> but an old commandment which ye had from the
> beginning. The old commandment is the word
> which ye have heard from the beginning."
>
> (I JOHN 2:7)

A dream—not unlike those
of the boy decades ago, silver-eyed
at an altar, wordless with awe,
in a village ruined yearly by rain.
There were twins
in the dream, red-haired children,
a boy and girl, a double creature

really, like those joined
at the hip in the womb. But, no,
it wasn't this, not only this,
but rather the dreaming itself
that was remarkable.
And also the presence
for a long part of the night
of the things young Dougherty gave me—
I mean, forgive me, my Goodnesses,
my great and lost love for the Dreamer.
And also the sense
of the thin rivulets of blood, running
up and down my legs
like commerce at a crossroads.
And the hearing of these veins clearly tingle—
yes, in fact, they rang.
And to say, *Ah Mary*—far more than once—
Mary, yes. It's so, Sister, it's so . . .

Witness in Aftershock

It's spring again, afternoon by now.
I see glass, so much glass; I see it
everywhere, and so much of it's hot
like it's come from the blowtube,
rubbery and red. The bubble's gone
too big and blown itself everywhere.
We'll never fix it.
No one will ever succeed in calling
the future up.
The roof of the opera house is on
the floor. I saw the lintel of the house
across the street—a glassen sidelong
mask of worked camellias—
shudder, then the house contract,
closing the jamb in on itself, and
the flowered transom shot out
of its frame and blew across
the street.
Life is a series of eleven-second bits.
Everyone living is at the wharf.
Glass is afire, flying, falling down.
There's a gash in my head; it's
singing, like glass does before it

breaks.
Awake, I'm putting bricks
in the pockets of my robe, calling
for Joshua, calling Victoria.
This is the coming of Truth,
she said; that's almost the last
I remember. Truth! Truth!
Joshy shouted, in horror, like the
truth had come from beyond in a wave
and would flatten the world at last
and all unlovely.
Truth, the god of war
and hater of the upright beam and
the crosswise rafter, had come!
Truth, like the breaker of glass—
but hasn't truth been under our feet
and hung before our eyes since forever,
common and colorless as the air?
No, it's the *shapes* of truth
that matter, and the coming of those
and their passing, and the great terror
they always bring.
I see a severed candlestick.
I cannot see the bay.
I am carrying a baby who was out,
sooty, walking alone through wreckage.
I remember Vicky's hair, her husband's
thick throat; also that last night
the carrion flower bloomed in the
greenhouse, stenching the air like
a dead dog's flesh; we couldn't
stand it. There was no moon.
And now there's black and red
everywhere.

I am bleeding on the child, stumbling
a way downhill toward the sirens
at last.
Someone's photo album's been
kicked down the street—the street's
been kicked down the street.
Roofs are down. My sister's missing.
And there are pictures of somebody's
family thrown everywhere on the
sudden rubbish.
I am walking down a carbon path
which is belabored with the walls
of homes; walking fallingly and
piecemeal, carrying a child on a
jackknife rumble of a road which has
been strewn with the faces
of people I may have been.

About the Author

Richard Ronan was born in 1946 in Jersey City, New Jersey and was raised there and in Damariscotta, Maine. He has since lived in Massachusetts, New Jersey and northern California. He attended parochial schools until college, completing his Master's work on Bashō and Wallace Stevens at the University of California, Berkeley.

He was the founder and has been the director for 14 years of a school for special high school students in western New Jersey, an activity which gained him Princeton University's Distinguished Teaching Award in 1980.

He is also the recipient of a Dodge Foundation grant to teach poetry and the winner of both the Emily Cook and Eisner poetry prizes. His prose, plays and poetry have appeared in many national publications, including the *American Poetry Review*.

His involvement with avant-garde theater has been long-standing. He has written and directed for several New York and New Jersey ensemble groups, including the Riverside Theatre Workshop and the Logos Company.

For the last five years he has divided his time between the New York and San Francisco Bay areas.

Cover design by Richard Haymes & Company, New York
Text design by Graywolf
Type (Sabon) set by Irish Setter, Portland
Manufactured by McNaughton & Gunn, Lithographers